In memory of Joseph Whitley, my maternal grandfather

Be it known that Joseph Whitley has been duly licensed by the Board of Police Commissioners of the City of Boston to be a Driver of Street Cars used in the streets of said City.
— City of Boston, Driver's License, Metropolitan Railroad Company, License No. 557, September 10, 1883 —

Joseph Whitley worked for the Metropolitan Railroad Company from 1883 to 1901, when he was reassigned to the Boston Elevated Railway Company. He worked for those Boston trolley car companies from 1883 until he passed away in 1927 at age 65.

For their help in making this book possible, I am indebted to Allison "Allie" Fiske, the little girl; Richard Lane, Jr., the grandfather; John Mazzei, the conductor; the trolley car passengers; Elizabeth Fiske, seamstress; and The Seashore Trolley Museum, including the director, Donald Curry, Judy Warner, and all the museum employees and volunteers.

First edition 1995

Library of Congress Cataloging-in-Publication Data.

McMillan, Bruce.
Grandfather's trolley / written and photo illustrated by Bruce McMillan.—1st ed.
Summary: A little girl remembers trolley rides with her grandfather, who was a trolley conductor.
ISBN 1-56402-633-7 (alk. paper)
[1. Trolley cars—Fiction. 2. Grandfathers—Fiction.] I. Title.
PZ7.M47878Gr 1995 [E]—dc20 95-10637

2 4 6 8 10 9 7 5 3 1

Printed in Belgium

Designed in part by Bruce McMillan

The book's photo-illustrations are representative of the color photographic techniques of the trolley era. They were shot and printed as black-and-white photographs, then toned brown, and finally hand tinted with oils.

Candlewick Press
2067 Massachusetts Avenue
Cambridge, Massachusetts 02140

GRANDFATHER'S TROLLEY

Written and photo-illustrated by Bruce McMillan

CANDLEWICK PRESS
CAMBRIDGE, MASSACHUSETTS

I remember . . .

When I was a little girl, I used to visit my grandfather at work. I waited and listened for the trolley.

ARUNDEL

Toot! Toot!

The trolley car rolled around
the bend. Grandfather was
the motorman.
"Hi, darlin'. Your seat's waitin'
for you. Hop aboard!"

I liked to sit way in back.
Grandfather always saved
a seat in the last row
— over the 8 —
just for me.

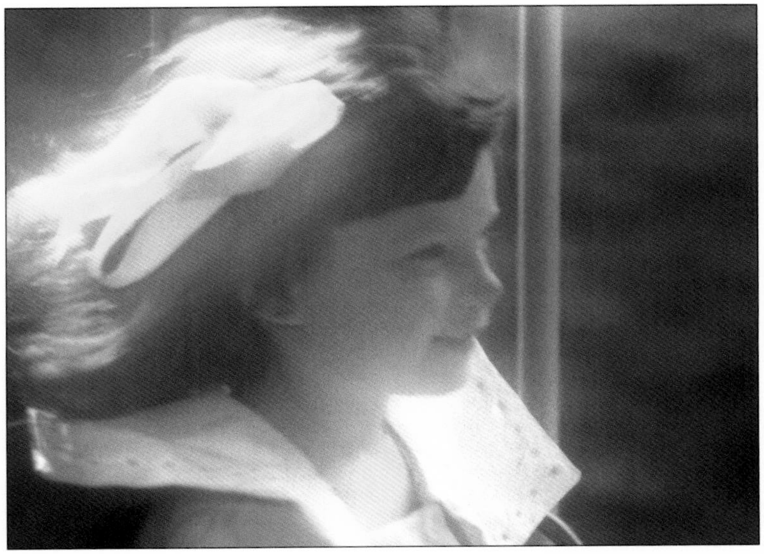

Ding ding!
Gong gong!

The trolley bells rang,
and we started
to move.

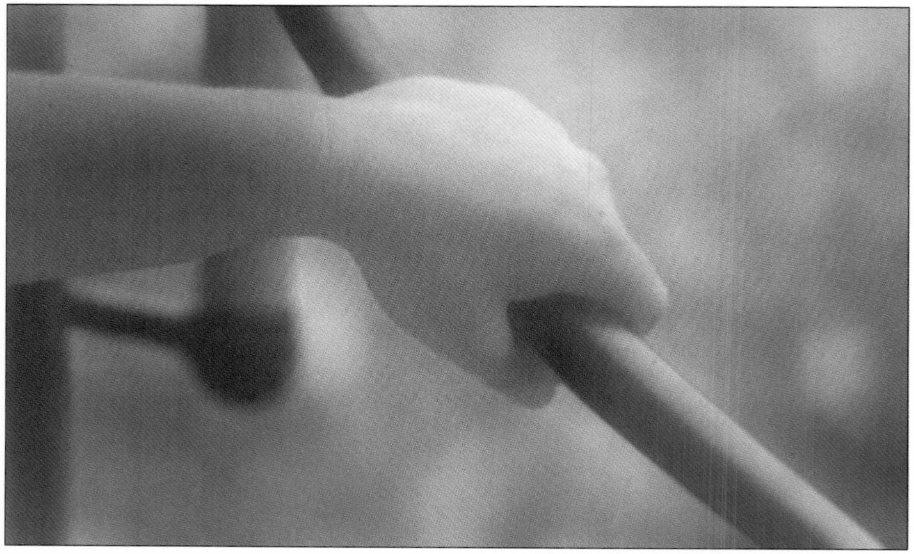

I held on tight. I pretended that I was motoring the trolley car, just like Grandfather.

Clackety-clackety, clackety-clack.

The woods sped by.

I leaned back and
squinted to keep the
breeze out of my eyes.
The trolley car swayed
from side to side.

Clackety-clackety,
clackety-clack.

I rocked with the car
from side to side.

Clackety-clackety,
clackety-clack.

At the end of the line,
Grandfather helped me down.
"Watch your step, darlin'.
Don't go too near the water."
Soon I heard him call, "All ready
for my number one helper!"

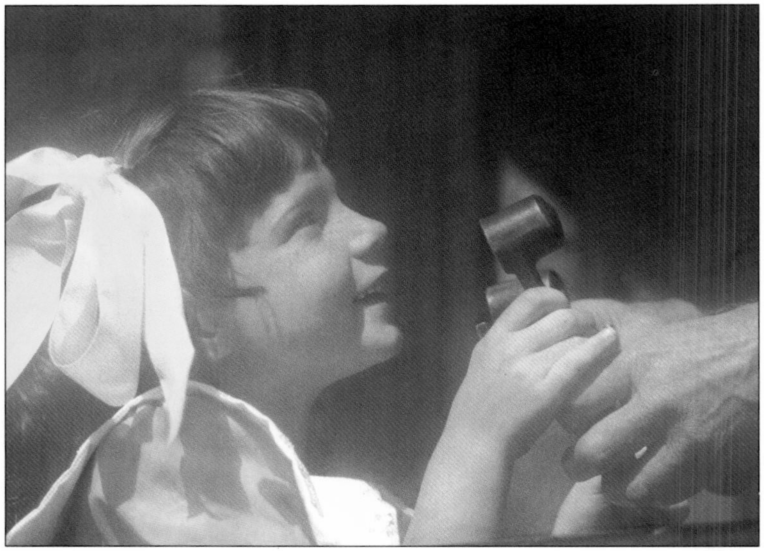

I brought the power
controls from one end
of the car to the other,
where Grandfather
was waiting.
"Thank you, number one."

The conductor
adjusted the trolley poles,
and the trolley car faced
back the way we'd come.
It was ready to go.

Ding ding! Gong gong!

On the ride back I sat up front
next to Grandfather.

Clackety-clackety, clackety-clack.

The wind blew hard.
Grandfather called back to me,
"I hope your hair ribbon's on tight!"

At the stop before mine,
Grandfather made room
for me by the controls.
Together, we motored
the trolley car.
Grandfather called out,
"Full speed ahead!"

***Clackety-clackety,
clackety-clack!***

The breeze blew by.
We sped along.
And then I saw my stop.

Grandfather
jumped off and
held out his arms.
"Free ride down for my
number one helper."
His whiskers tickled
when I hugged him.
I said, "Thank you,
Grandfather."

Before he started
the trolley again,
Grandfather watched
me run home down
the lane. I never had
to look back to see if
he was watching me.
I just knew. . . .

He was my grandfather.

A Note from the Author

The trolley car in this book, Connecticut Trolley 838, was built in 1905 by J. M. Jones Sons, West Troy, New York. Its last Connecticut runs transported football fans to and from the Yale Bowl in 1946. In 1975 the car was fully restored by the Seashore Trolley Museum, located near Kennebunkport, Maine. It remains there today, and because this is a working museum, visitors may still ride on trolley car 838.

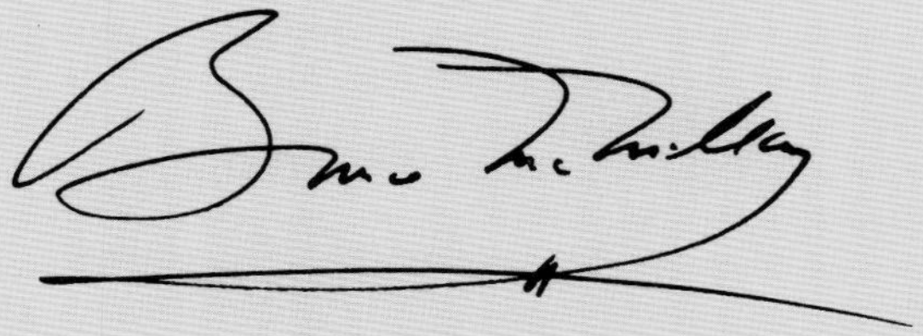